D0482686

DATE DUE

JUL 2 6 2005		
JUL 0 9 11		

3 1853 01324 3030

ABOUT THE BANK STREET READY-TO-READ SERIES

Seventy years of educational research and innovative teaching have given the Bank Street College of Education the reputation as America's most trusted name in early childhood education.

Because no two children are exactly alike in their development, we have designed the *Bank Street Ready-to-Read* series in three levels to accommodate the individual stages of reading readiness of children ages four through eight.

- ○ *Level 1:* GETTING READY TO READ—read-alouds for children who are taking their first steps toward reading.
- ● *Level 2:* READING TOGETHER—for children who are just beginning to read by themselves but may need a little help.
- ○ *Level 3:* I CAN READ IT MYSELF—for children who can read independently.

Our three levels make it easy to select the books most appropriate for a child's development and enable him or her to grow with the series step by step. The *Bank Street Ready-to-Read* books also overlap and reinforce each other, further encouraging the reading process.

We feel that making reading fun and enjoyable is the single most important thing that you can do to help children become good readers. And we hope you'll be a part of Bank Street's long tradition of learning through sharing.

The Bank Street College
of Education

For William, the lion,
and Molly, the lamb
— W.H.H.

For Leland
— B.B.

For Paul Hallenbeck:
a gentleman, and the hardest-working
man in Rhinebeck
— B.D.

For a free color catalog describing Gareth Stevens' list of high-quality books and multimedia programs, call 1-800-542-2595 (USA) or 1-800-461-9120 (Canada). Gareth Stevens Publishing's Fax: (414) 225-0377.

Library of Congress Cataloging-in-Publication Data

Brenner, Barbara.
    Ups and downs with Lion and Lamb / by Barbara Brenner and William H. Hooks; illustrated by Bruce Degen.
        p. cm. -- (Bank Street ready-to-read)
        Summary: In three episodes, Lion and Lamb start their own club, go on a picnic, and see their friendship threatened by Lion's forced move with his family.
        ISBN 0-8368-1783-4 (lib. bdg.)
        [1. Lions--Fiction. 2. Sheep--Fiction. 3. Friendship--Fiction.] I. Hooks, William H. II. Degen, Bruce, ill. III. Title. IV. Series.
    PZ7.B7518Up 1999
    [E]--dc21   98-38484

This edition first published in 1999 by
Gareth Stevens Publishing
1555 North RiverCenter Drive, Suite 201
Milwaukee, Wisconsin 53212 USA

© 1991 by Byron Preiss Visual Publications, Inc. Text © 1991 by Bank Street College of Education. Illustrations © 1991 by Bruce Degen and Byron Preiss Visual Publications, Inc.

Printed in Mexico

1 2 3 4 5 6 7 8 9 03 02 01 00 99

Bank Street Ready-to-Read™

Ups and Downs with Lion and Lamb

by Barbara Brenner and William H. Hooks
Illustrated by Bruce Degen

A Byron Preiss Book

Gareth Stevens Publishing
MILWAUKEE

CONTENTS

MEMBERS ONLY

Lamb walked over to Bear's house.
There was a big sign on the door:

KEEP OUT
MEMBERS ONLY

"That's strange," said Lamb.
"Who does Bear want to keep out?"

Lamb walked around to the window.
She looked inside.
There was Bear with Wolf, Lion,
and Tiger.
They were shouting
and waving their arms in the air.
Lamb listened.

"The club was my idea," said Tiger.
"So I should be president."
"I'm the biggest and strongest,"
growled Bear.
"So I should be president."
"I never get to be anything," cried Wolf.
"I want to be president."

"Stop!" roared Lion.

"I have to be president."

"Why?" asked Wolf.

"Because lions are always president," said Lion.

Then they all shouted at once.

Lamb opened the door and walked in.

"Hi, everybody," she said.

Lion, Wolf, Tiger, and Bear
stopped talking.
"Well," said Lamb, "what's new?"
Wolf said, "Out!"
and pointed to the door.
Lamb stood still.

"Out! Out!" shouted Tiger and Bear.
Lamb looked at Lion.
Lion hung his head.
"Members only," he said softly.
"Please, pretty please," said Lamb.
"Out!" they all shouted together.

Lamb turned and left.
She slammed the door behind her.
Lamb was mad.
"Who needs their old club anyway?"
she said.
"I'll form my own club.
And I know just the place for it."

So Lamb went to a cave in the woods.
It was a secret place
that only she and Lion knew about.
She found a board and wrote:

LAMBS CLUB

She put the sign in front of the cave.
Then she brought a basket of peanuts,
a jug of water, and a big, soft pillow.
"Now, this is a real cozy club,"
said Lamb.
"I think I'll take a nap."

When Lamb woke up,
Lion was sitting in front of the cave.
"I knew I would find you here,"
he said.
Lion started to enter the cave.
"Out!" said Lamb.
She pointed to the sign on the cave.

"Why can't I come in?" asked Lion.
"Are you a lamb?" asked Lamb.
"No," he said.
"Well, what does the sign say?"
she asked.
"I can read," said Lion.

"Besides, you have your own club,"
said Lamb.

"The club broke up," he said sadly.

"Why?" Lamb asked.

"We couldn't decide who should be
president."

"Too bad," said Lamb.

She started eating peanuts.

Lion's mouth began to water.

"Do you allow visitors to your club?"
he asked.
"Only lambs," answered Lamb.
"Aw, come on," said Lion.
"Lambs only," said Lamb.
"Please," said Lion.

Lamb stopped eating peanuts.

"Did you say, 'Please' ?"

"Pretty please," said Lion with a gulp.

"Now you're acting like a lamb,"
said Lamb.

"Come on in, pussycat.
Have some peanuts."

"Thanks," said Lion.

He took a big pawful of peanuts.

"Well," said Lamb, "shall we talk about who is going to be president?"

"No," said Lion.

"Let's just eat peanuts."

THE LOST ROAR

Lion was waiting for Lamb.
"Lamb is never late,"
he said to himself.
"Never for a picnic."
Lion checked his backpack.
One double Leoburger.
Mmmm—did it smell good!
A bag of hot buttered popcorn.
"I'll just have one piece," said Lion.
"*Mmmm*—well, maybe two."

Lion had eaten half the popcorn
when he saw Lamb running up the road.
"Hi, pussycat," she called.
"Sorry I'm late."
"Where's your backpack?" asked Lion.
"We're going on a picnic, remember?"

"I remember," said Lamb.
"But I can't go."
"First you keep me waiting," said Lion.
"Then you tell me you can't go.
Some friend you are."
"I have to look after my little sister,
Lambkin, today," said Lamb.
"Lambkin, Lambkin.
That's all I ever hear!" Lion said.
"She spoils everything."

"Maybe we *can* have our picnic,"
said Lamb.
"How?" asked Lion.
"We can take Lambkin with us."
"Oh, no," groaned Lion.
"Lions don't baby-sit."

"Lambkin will sleep the whole time.
You'll forget she's there," said Lamb.
"Besides, I made your favorite food."
"Double chocolate people crackers?"
asked Lion.
"It would be a shame to waste them,"
said Lamb.
"Okay. Lambkin can come," said Lion.

So Lion and Lamb and Lambkin
set out for their picnic.
Lambkin skipped along in front,
singing "Baa, baa black sheep."

As soon as they reached the pond,
Lambkin ate two people crackers
and went right to sleep.
"Let's play Stick Chase
before we eat," said Lion.
"Great idea," said Lamb.
"But we can't go too far.
I have to keep an eye on Lambkin."
"Always Lambkin," muttered Lion.

Lion threw a stick near the water.
"Race you for that stick!" he cried.
Lion got there first.
He waved the stick in the air.

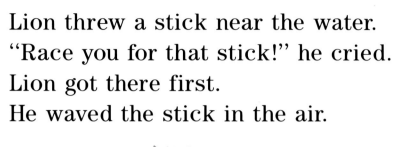

Then he threw it
into a bunch of cattails.
"Race again," he yelled.
Lamb ran as fast as she could.
She reached the cattails before Lion
and found the stick.

"We're even now!" she cried.
Then she threw the stick.
It landed in a thorn patch.
They raced toward the thorn patch.

Suddenly Lamb stopped.
"Lambkin is crying," she said.
Lion kept running after the stick.
Lamb ran back toward Lambkin.
"Help! Help!" Lamb cried.
"A wolf is stealing Lambkin!"

Lion stopped.
He saw the big wolf pick up Lambkin.
Lamb rushed back to Lion.
"Roar! Roar!" she cried.
"Your roar will scare off the wolf."

Lion didn't roar.
"Roar!" Lamb shouted.
"I can't," he said.
"I lose my roar when I'm afraid."
Lamb couldn't believe her ears.
She quickly broke a long thorn
from one of the thornbushes.
"Lion," she said, "this is going to
hurt me more than it hurts you."

Then she pricked Lion with the thorn.
"ROARRRR! ROARRRR!"
cried Lion as he jumped into the air.
The wolf heard the loud roar
and saw Lion jump.
He dropped Lambkin
and ran off into the woods.

Lamb ran to her little sister.
"There, there, Lambkin," she said.
"Brave Lion saved you from the wolf."
Lambkin stopped crying.
She walked over to Lion.
"Can I give you a hug, brave Lion?"
she asked.

"Well—" said Lion.
He looked all around.
No one was in sight.
"Oh, all right," Lion said.
"But it's got to be our secret.
Lions don't go around hugging lambs."
Lamb smiled and began to unpack
their picnic lunch.

MOVING

Lamb was in the meadow playing.
Lion came along, looking gloomy.
"Hi, Lion," Lamb called.
"Want to play Chase-Your-Tail?"
Lion shook his head.
"You'd better ask Dog."
"Good idea!" said Lamb.
"We can all play."
"Not after today, we can't," said Lion.
"Why not, pussycat?" asked Lamb.
"I'll be gone," said Lion.
"We're moving."

"Moving?" asked Lamb. "But why?"

"Lions need a lot of space," said Lion.

"There's a big space
in the next meadow," said Lamb.

"We're not moving there," said Lion.
"We're moving far away."

"Just where are you moving?"
asked Lamb.

Lion cleared his throat.
"All the way across the water."
"You mean the ocean?" Lamb cried.
"You must be moving to Africa!"
"I told you it was far," Lion said sadly.
"I guess this is good-bye, Lamb,"
he said, holding out his paw.
"I'll never have another friend
like you."

"Good-bye, Lion," said Lamb
in a trembly voice.
"I'll never have another friend
like you," she said.
"Yes, you will," sighed Lion.
"You'll have Dog."

The next day Lamb was taking
a lonely walk.
Along came Dog.
"Where are you going, Lamb?"
he asked.
"Down to the river to think," she said.
"I'll just tag along," said Dog.
"What are we thinking about?"
"We're thinking about Lion,"
said Lamb.
"I miss him so much."
"Really?" asked Dog. "He just left."

Lamb sighed and gazed
across the river.
Something moved in the grass.
"Do you see what I see?" she asked.
"It looks like a big cat," said Dog.
"It looks like a lion," said Lamb.
"Another one?" said Dog.
"I didn't know there were so many
lions around here."

They watched as the lion came closer.
"He looks just like our lion,"
said Lamb.
"All lions look alike," said Dog.
"But it can't be our lion," said Lamb.
"He's on his way to Africa."
"And I'm on my way home," said Dog.
He hurried away.

The lion roared across the river.
"Is that a lamb I see?"
"Of course I'm a lamb," said Lamb.
"Don't you know a lamb
when you see one?"
"Indeed, I do," said the lion.
"My best friend was a lamb.
But I didn't know there were lambs
in Africa."
Lamb burst out laughing.
"Lion, it's me.
Don't you know your best friend?"

"What are you doing in Africa?"
asked Lion.
"You're not in Africa," Lamb said.
"But I moved across the water,"
said Lion.
"You moved to the other side
of the *river*."

"You mean I didn't move far away?"
"Not far at all," said Lamb.
"I'm so happy, pussycat.
Now, come over here
so I can give you a hug."
Lion came over.